14.95

SLEEPING BEAUTY

THE BALLET STORY

SLEEPING BEAUTY

THE BALLET STORY

RETOLD BY MARIAN HOROSKO

ILLUSTRATED BY TODD L. W. DONEY

ATHENEUM 1994 NEW YORK

MAXWELL MACMILLAN CANADA Toronto
MAXWELL MACMILLAN INTERNATIONAL New York Oxford Singapore Sydney

*O*nce upon a time, a princess was born in a kingdom beyond the sea. Her parents, the king and queen, called the baby Aurora, which means "morning light."

Our story begins with Aurora's christening. Everyone has been invited to the celebration in the throne room of the castle. Aurora is in her tiny cradle; a soft canopy hangs over her head. Two nurses guard her. Cattalabutte, the servant in charge of welcoming the king's guests, is busy checking his list and bowing to cavaliers and maids of honor as they enter. They pass the cradle to admire Aurora in her long, white christening dress.

Trumpets are heard. It is a fanfare announcing the arrival of Aurora's father and mother, King Florestan and the queen. They circle the room, greeting the members of the court, and then sit on their thrones to await their special guests, Aurora's fairy godmothers.

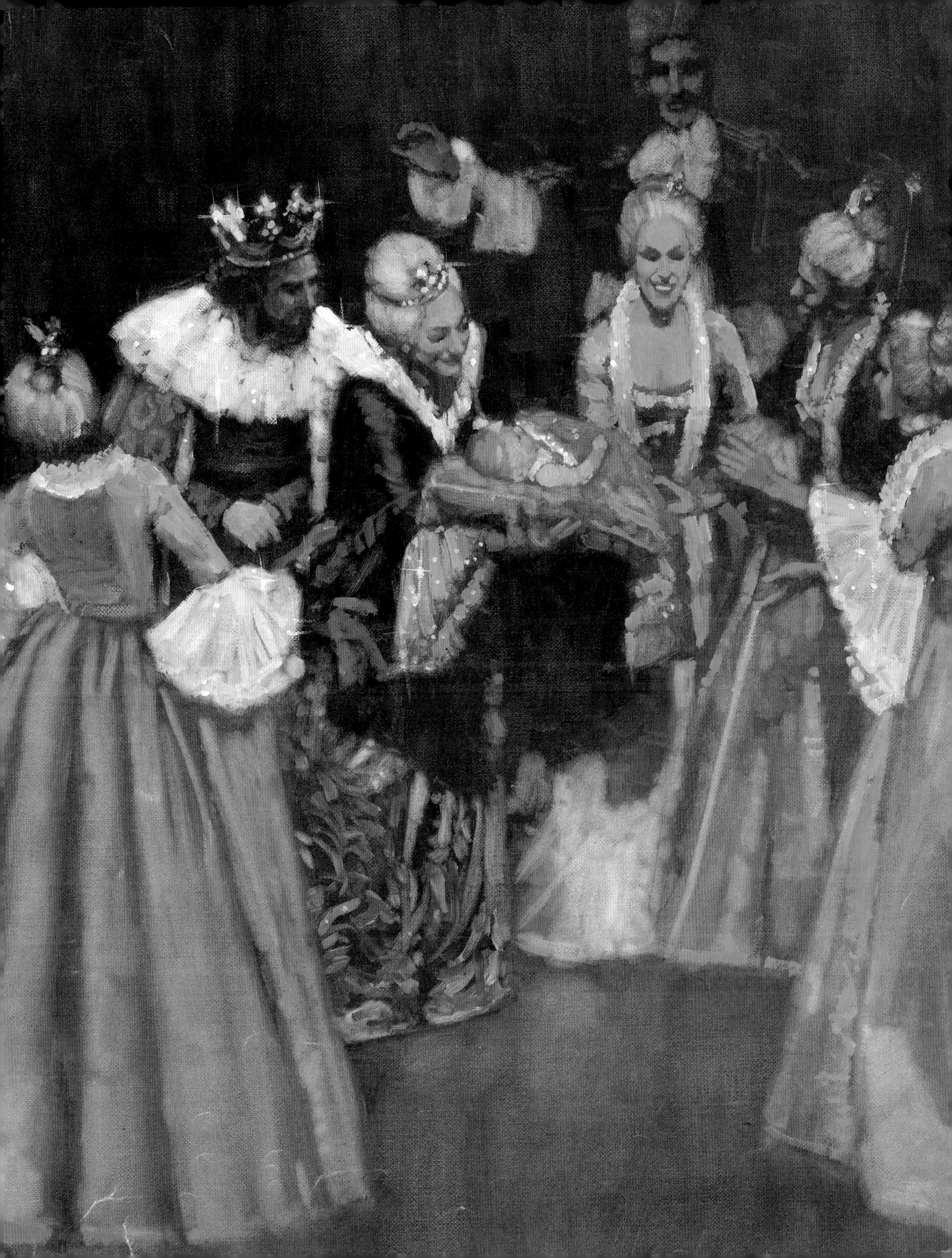

A run on the harp signals the approach of the Lilac Fairy with five companions, Aurora's godmothers. They have come to bless her with lovely virtues: tenderness, vivacity, generosity, eloquence, and courage. The most powerful godmother, the Lilac Fairy, protects Aurora from harm.

The Fairy of the Crystal Fountain bestows the gift of tenderness with a short dance with gentle movements. The Fairy of the Enchanted Garden gives Aurora vivacity, danced with swift turns, or pirouettes. The Fairy of the Woodland Glades, who offers generosity, dances slowly and quietly. The Fairy of the Songbirds flits across the stage. Her music tinkles, and in a flash she chirps eloquence and flies away. Courage is given to Aurora by the Fairy of the Golden Vine. She points her index fingers in every direction to punch the air with energy.

At last, the Lilac Fairy comes forward and performs a lovely waltz with flowing movements. Although she will fly away, she will always return when Aurora needs her.

All the guests join in a dance of celebration, until a terrible noise makes them stop to listen. It seems to come from outside the castle.

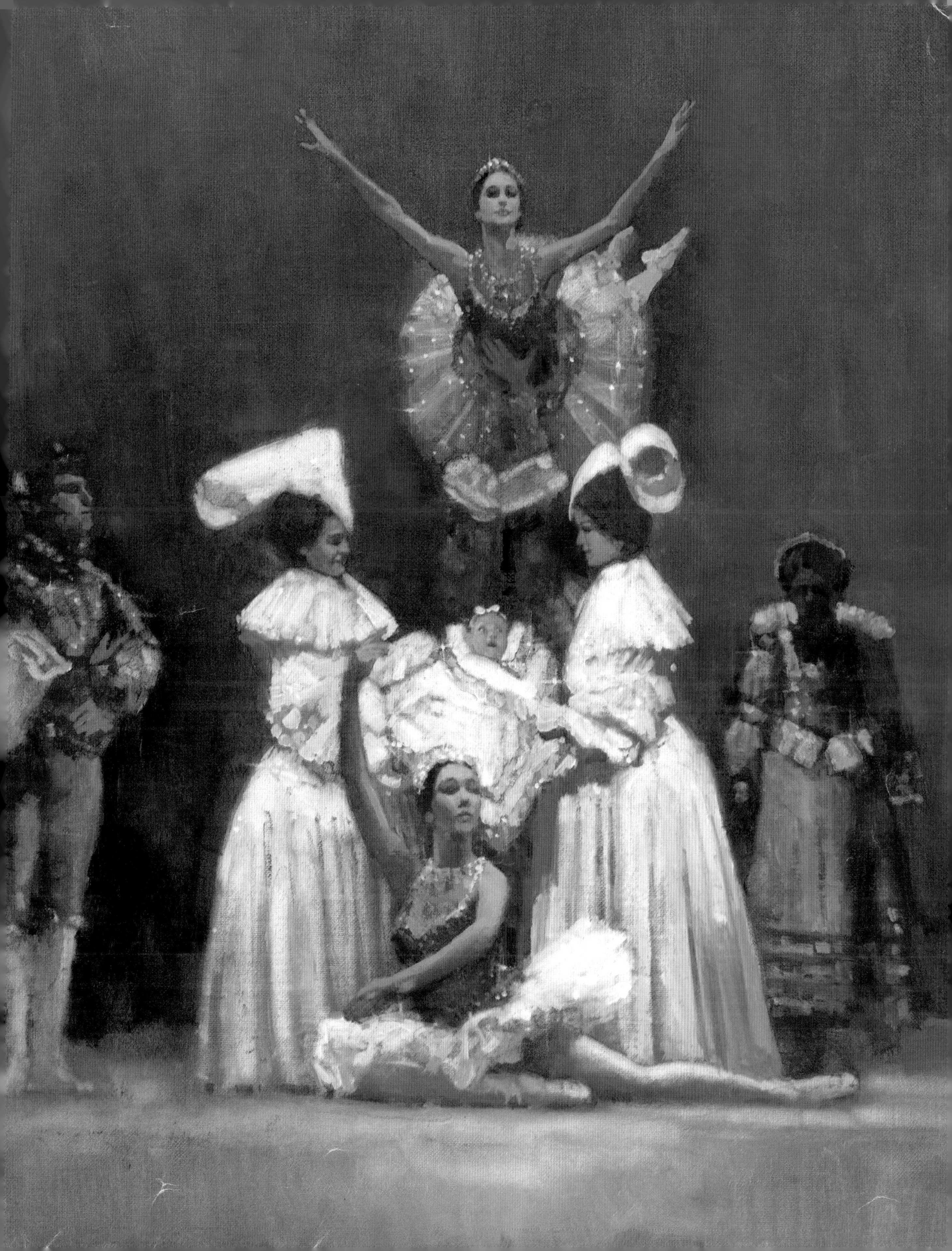

*T*he king rushes down from his throne to investigate. Suddenly, two giant rats enter the room and make threatening movements that frighten all the guests. The king understands what has happened, but it is too late to make amends. Cattalabutte, his servant, has forgotten to invite the evil fairy, the hideous and nasty Carabosse. What a blunder!

A black coach drawn by four more huge rats dashes into the throne room. Carabosse is inside. She is furious and will surely do harm. The entire kingdom is in peril.

The coach stops, and Carabosse steps out in her long black dress and hobbles forward on her stick. "Why was I not invited?" she asks in pantomime.

The king points to the culprit—Cattalabutte! Carabosse reaches out with her long fingernails and snatches Cattalabutte's wig from his head to disgrace him. But that does not make up for his mistake of not inviting her. She caresses her ugly rats and does a grotesque dance, then places a curse on the princess. "When the princess grows up," she seems to say, "she will be the most beautiful princess of all; and then"—she points to the princess with her stick—"she will die." The evil fairy cackles. "She will prick her finger on a spindle, and then she will be a beautiful dead princess!"

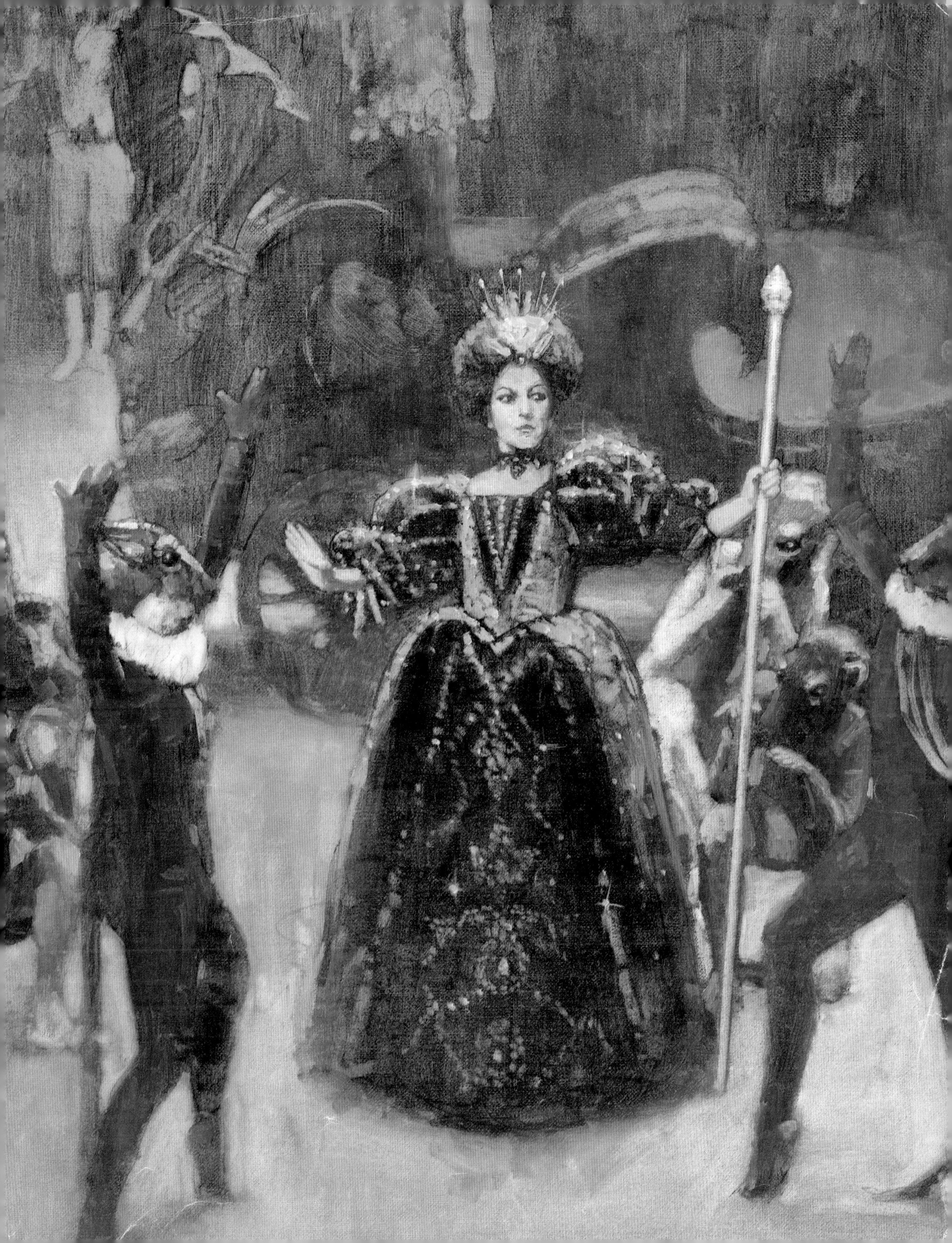

The good fairies beg her to change her mind. But no, Carabosse persists in laughing at the dismay of the king and queen and whips her great black cape through the air.

The Lilac Fairy steps out to prevent Carabosse from approaching too near the cradle as the other fairies gather around to protect Aurora. Carabosse shakes her stick, but the Lilac Fairy has raised her magic wand against her. The evil fairy staggers back, dances her final, frantic jig, and climbs back into her black coach, shaking her fists at the entire court as she rides off with her monsters.

But Aurora will be protected. For, you see, the Lilac Fairy has not yet bestowed her gift. A lovely melody calms the royal house as the Lilac Fairy assures the court that Aurora will only *seem* to die, but instead, she will be asleep—asleep for one hundred years. And all the court will sleep, too. But one day, a handsome prince who loves Aurora will awaken her with a kiss, and everyone will live happily ever after.

The king and the queen are relieved and grateful to the Lilac Fairy. As the curtain falls, the queen stands over her daughter in the cradle. The fairies and the court gather round to protect the child from the evil fairy's curse.

CURTAIN

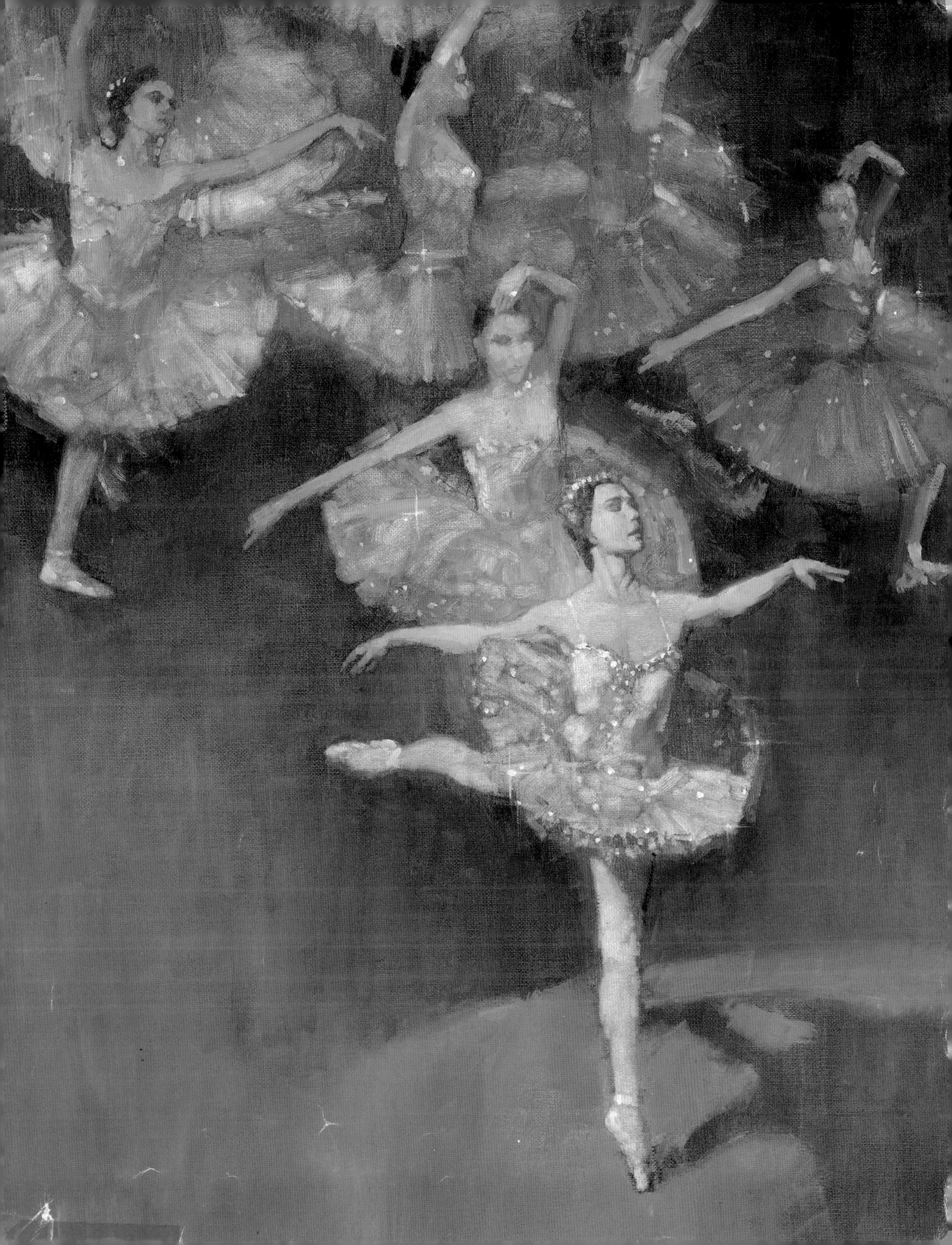

THE SPELL

Sixteen years have passed, and it is Aurora's birthday. Ladies-in-waiting with their cavaliers walk about admiring the palace garden. Peasants, a short distance away, are celebrating the princess's birthday, too. Everyone is anxious to see the four princes from England, India, Italy, and Spain who have come to seek the hand of the young princess.

But in a corner of the garden lurk three hags, with black hoods around their faces and spindles in their hands. Spindles have been banned in this kingdom because of the wicked fairy's curse. But there they are. Cattalabutte sees them and is not going to let the hags get away. The old master of ceremonies catches them and grabs one of their spindles.

At that very moment, the king and queen arrive with the four princes, and in the excitement, one of the women escapes into a corner.

The king sees that Cattalabutte is hiding something behind his back and demands to know what it is. A spindle! The king is furious and commands the culprits to come before him. The hags cower in fear of punishment for disobeying his rule and beg for his forgiveness as the king, wanting to protect his daughter, begins to pronounce his sentence. The queen interrupts. "It is, after all," she gestures, "Aurora's birthday, and the women seem sorry." The king lets the old women go.

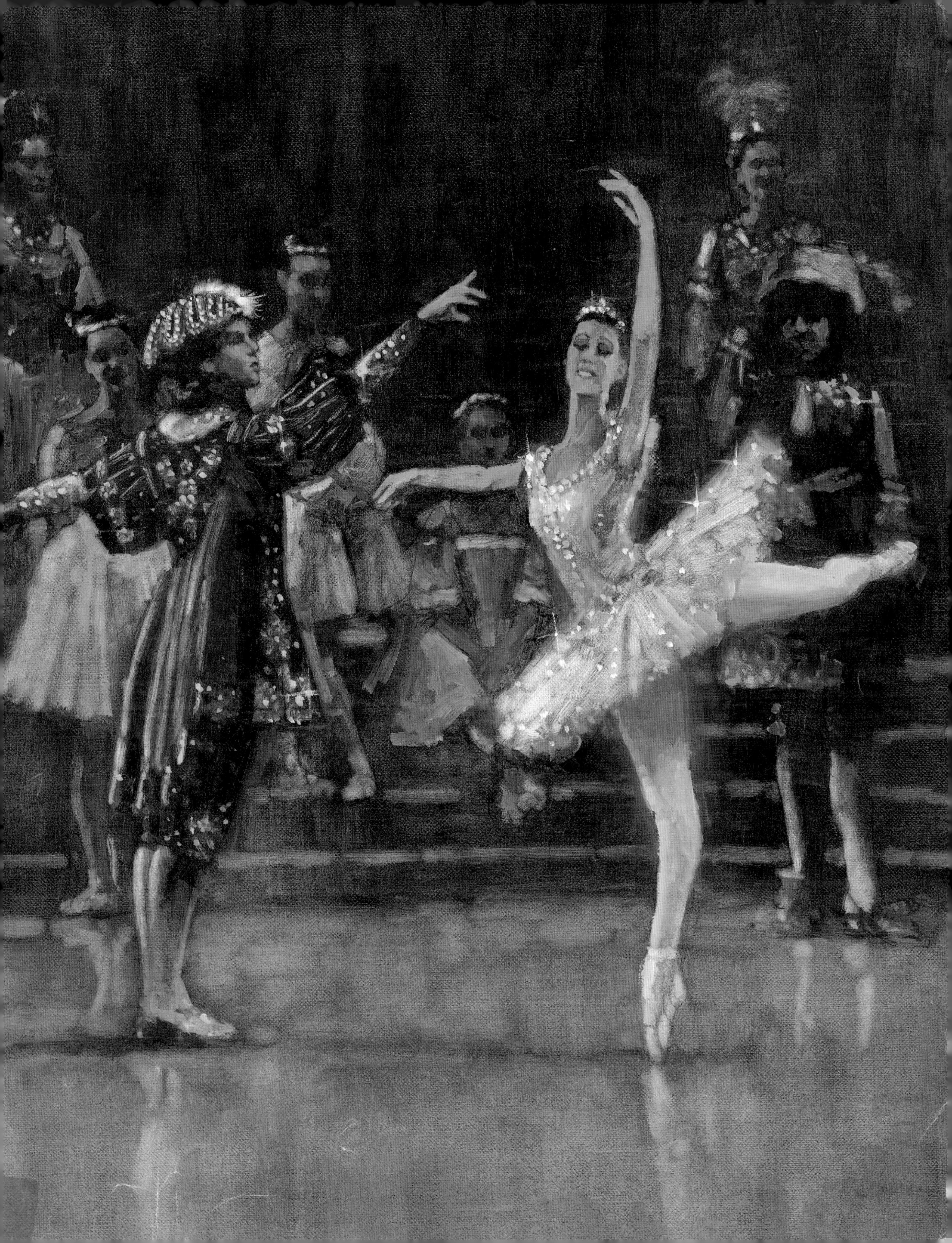

*T*he birthday party goes on as young peasants dance cheerfully. Musicians and young friends of the princess arrive. The four princes are presented and wait to greet the princess. Aurora appears in her beautiful pink birthday dress and does a short dance filled with happiness and expectation.

Then she is introduced to her four suitors. Each prince becomes her partner in a slow dance. As they dance with her, each prince gives her a red rose. When she has all four roses, she offers the bouquet to her mother.

Her mother encourages her to dance again and Aurora is so filled with happiness that she leaps even higher and faster than before. Her joy gives pleasure to all the court.

At that moment the third woman, who had kept herself hidden until now, sidles up and holds out her present to the princess. Aurora accepts the gift. It is a strange, new object. A spindle! The king rushes down from his throne to save his daughter, but it is too late. Aurora is charmed by the spindle and playfully twirls it around until she pricks her finger.

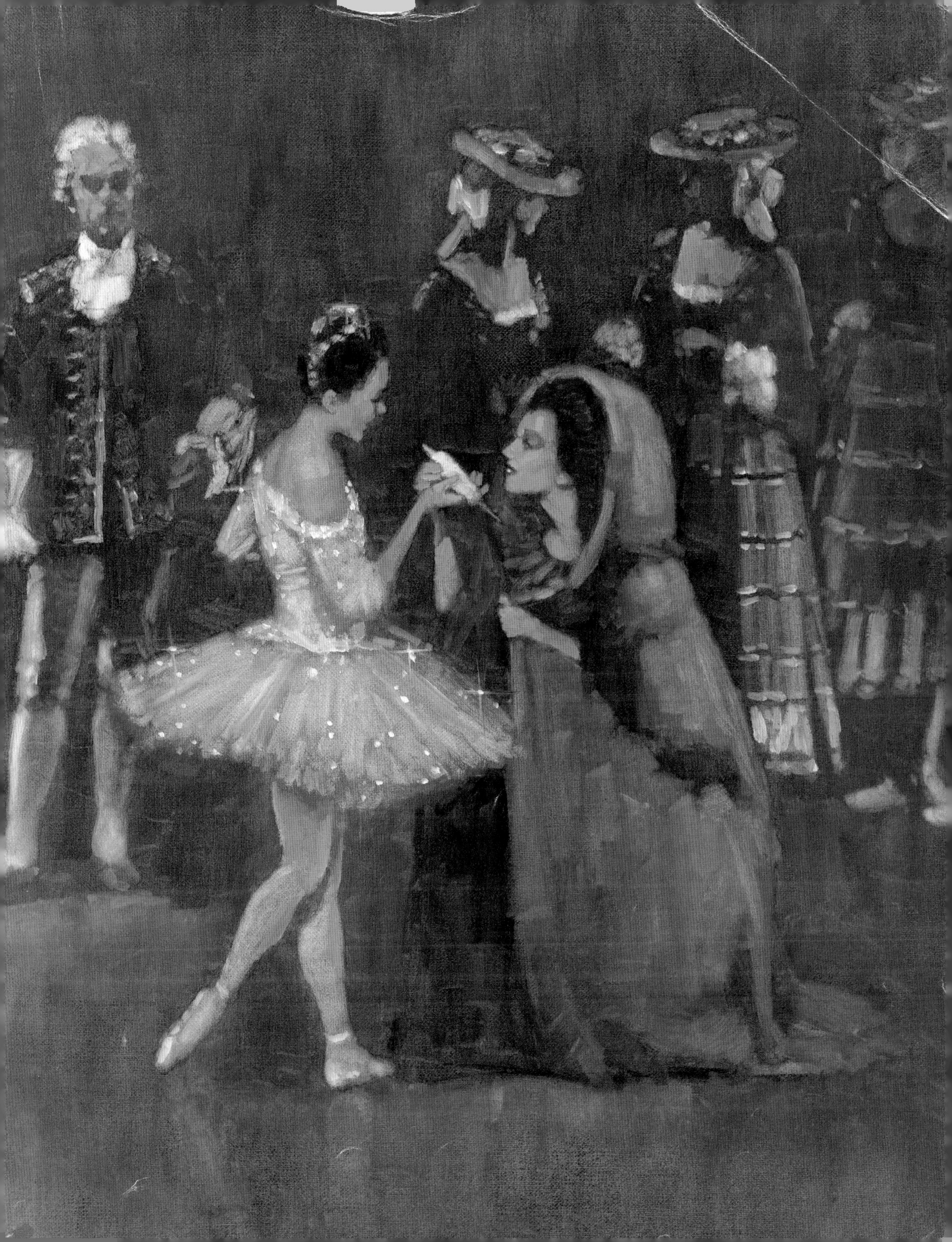

At first, she looks puzzled, then begins to sway. She tries to assure her parents that she has not been harmed and struggles to dance. But it is no use. There is a burst of thunder, and Aurora faints into her father's arms.

The entire court is in a panic. Cymbals clash and the old woman who gave Aurora the spindle appears from the crowd. She throws aside her cape so that all may see she is the evil fairy, Carabosse, who has come to fulfill her prophecy. Armed courtiers chase her into the garden. There is confusion and dismay.

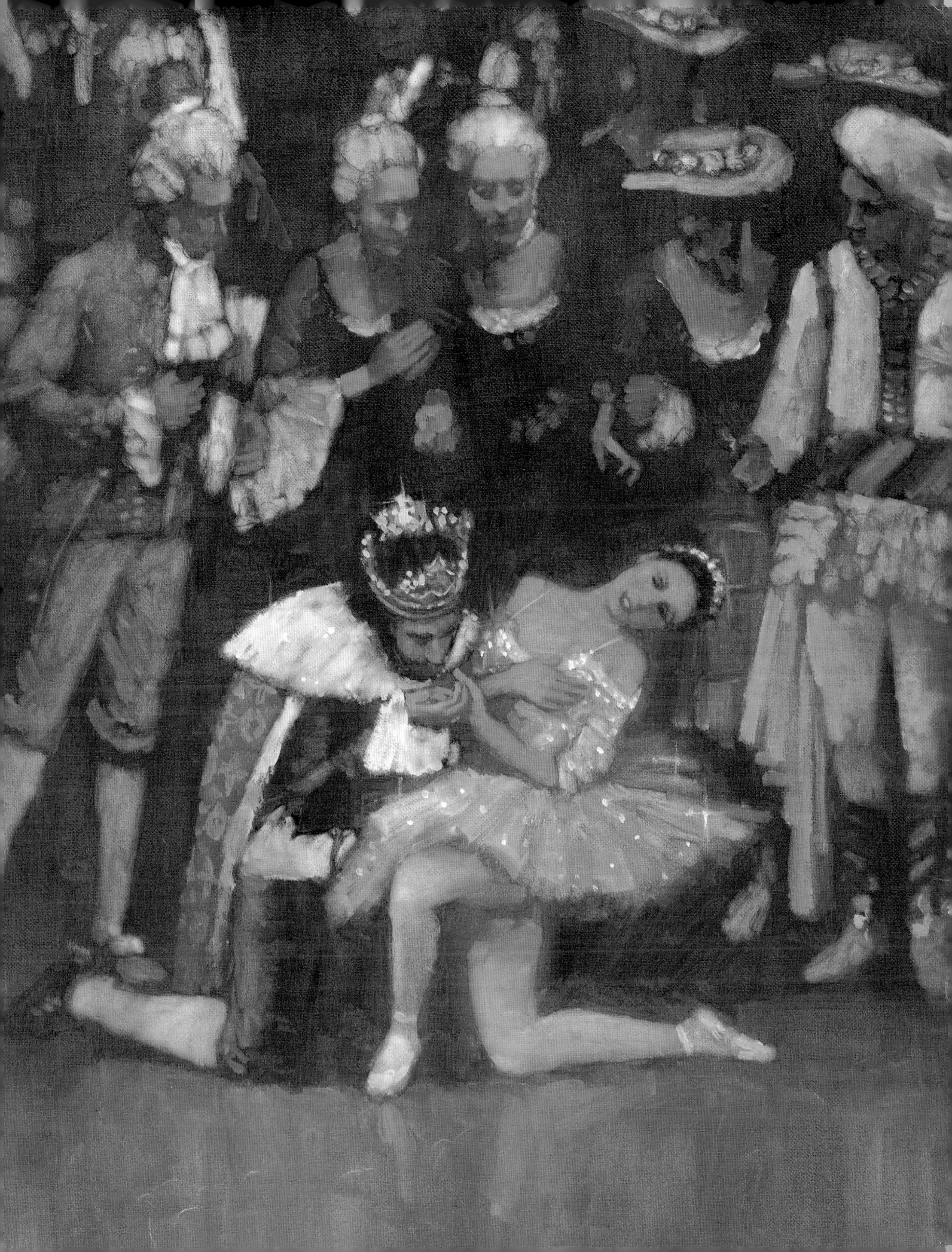

$\mathcal{A}$ trumpet is heard that silences everyone. Then a harp signals the arrival of the Lilac Fairy. True to her promise of protection, she arrives and assures the king and queen that the princess is not dead, but will only sleep for one hundred years. Slowly, the princess is carried up the steps to the bedchamber where members of the court lie down around her. The Lilac Fairy waves them to sleep with her wand.

It grows dark; the garden fades; and enormous shrubs and trees with huge branches begin to cover the palace. But the Lilac Fairy can still be seen as she protects the court in their sleep of one hundred years.

CURTAIN

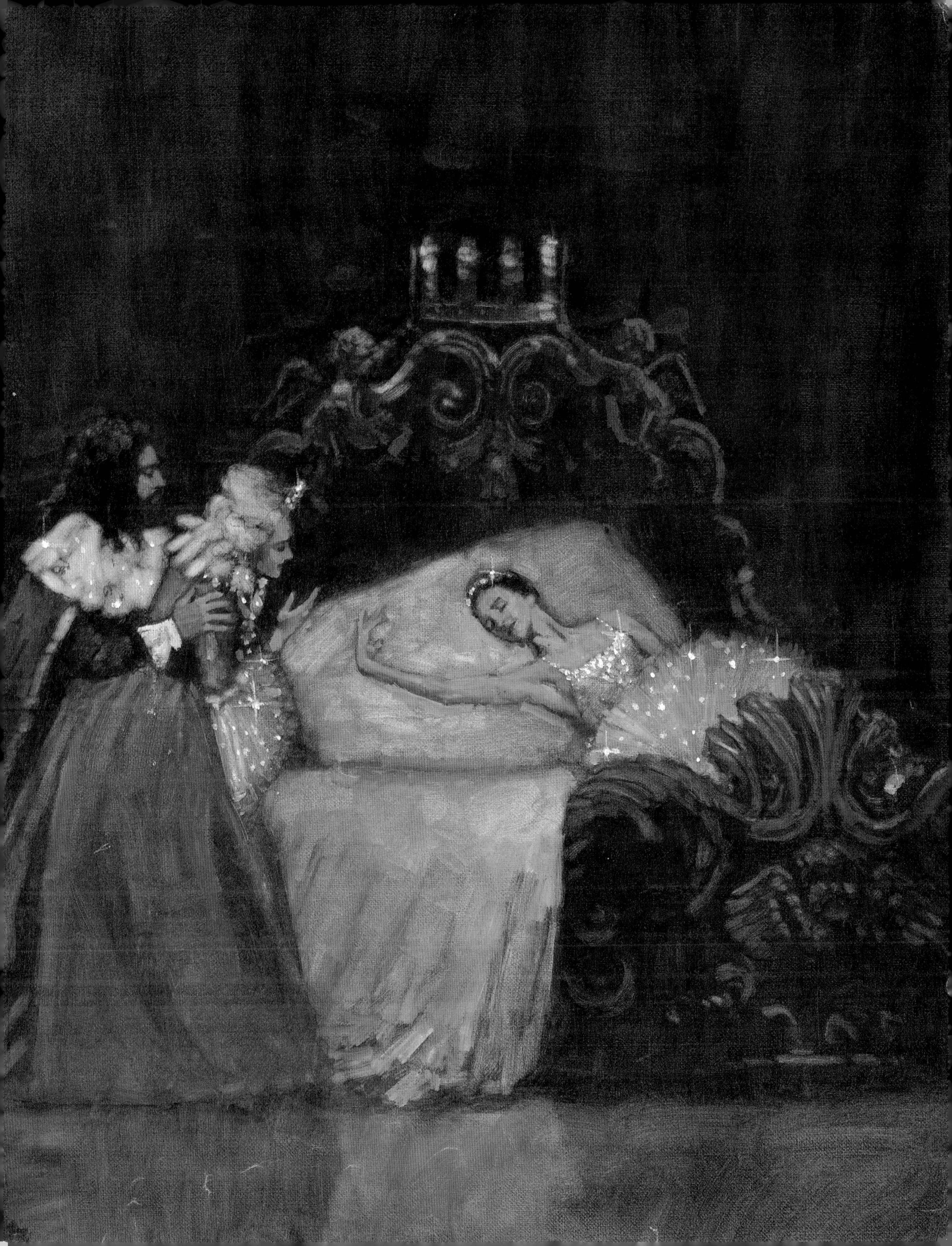

THE VISION

The sound of hunting horns is heard, and the curtain rises on a forest one hundred years later. Prince Florimund, handsome but melancholy—unhappy—finds he is not amused by the members of his court, especially not by a young countess who considers herself the prince's special friend.

The group plays a game of blindman's bluff with the prince's old tutor but that fails to distract Florimund. He dances a stately mazurka with the countess, but even that does not please him. The peasants dance, too. The prince is gracious, but not cheered. Servants bring hunting weapons. The prince still remains distracted and sad, but doesn't know why. He dismisses the court; he wants to be alone.

Alone now, the prince stares into the lovely lake nearby, hoping that its beauty will lift his gloom. He does not see the Lilac Fairy's seashell boat gliding toward him.

He is startled when the boat lands on the shore, but soon remembers his manners and bows courteously to the Lilac Fairy. She asks him if his heart is free. He says it is, and she tells him of a beautiful sleeping princess, who will sleep forever unless she is kissed and awakened by a prince who truly loves her.

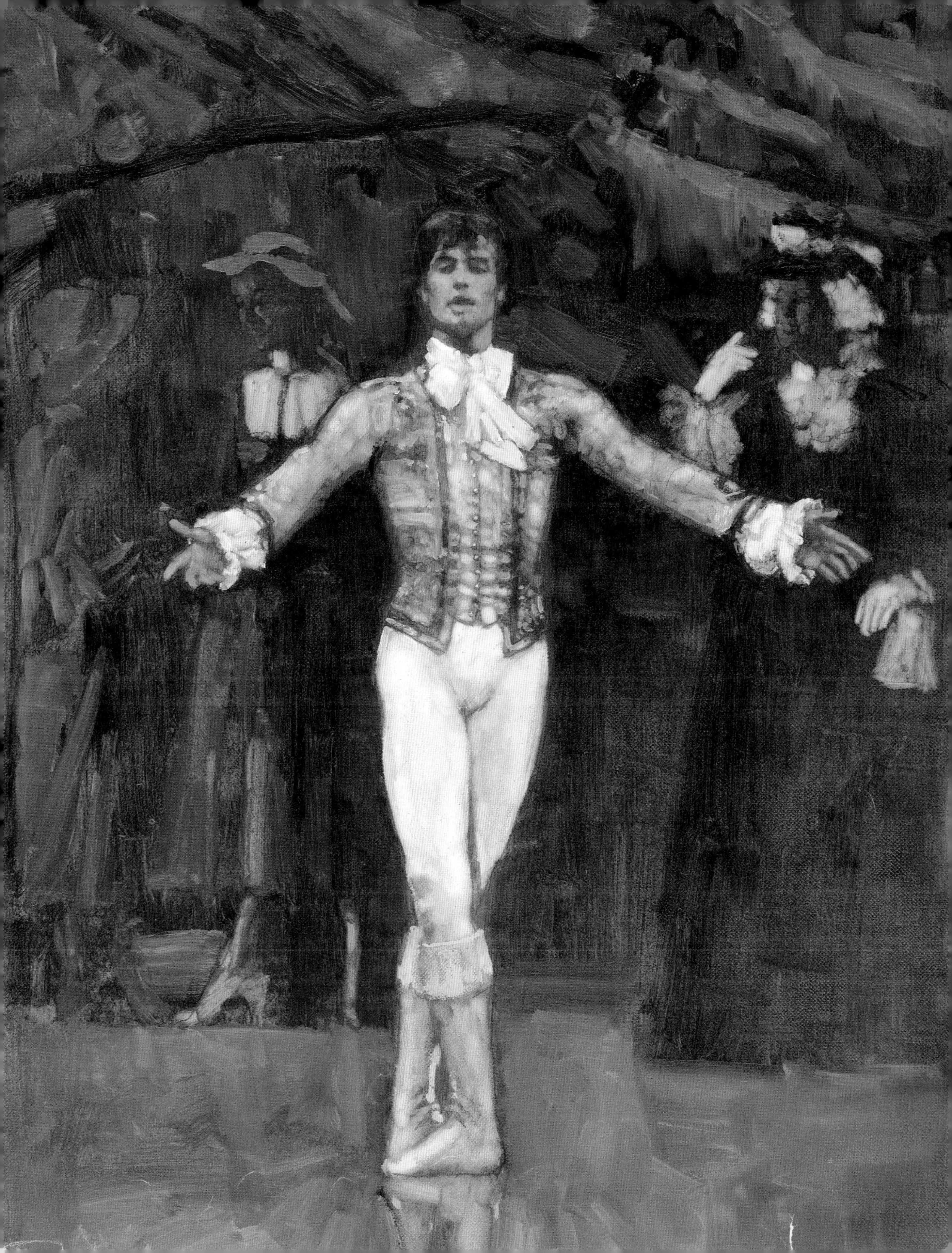

The prince doesn't quite believe the Lilac Fairy. "Show me this beautiful princess," he seems to say. The fairy waves her wand, and a vision of the princess appears in the forest amid the trees.

The princess is only a vision, but the prince is enthralled as she dances to soft music. He comes close and lifts her high in the air, but as soon as he puts her down, she disappears, surrounded by nymphs who keep the prince from capturing his vision of Aurora. Prince Florimund is determined to find the princess of the vision, for he has fallen in love with her.

"Where is the real Aurora?" the prince seems to ask. The Lilac Fairy beckons him to her seashell boat. The way is long and the road difficult, but at the end, the prince will find his princess.

Away they sail until they land on a mysterious shore. The Lilac Fairy leads him into woods covered with the vines, branches, and cob-webs of one hundred years. The prince slashes through them with his sword, and finally, before him, he sees a lovely old palace.

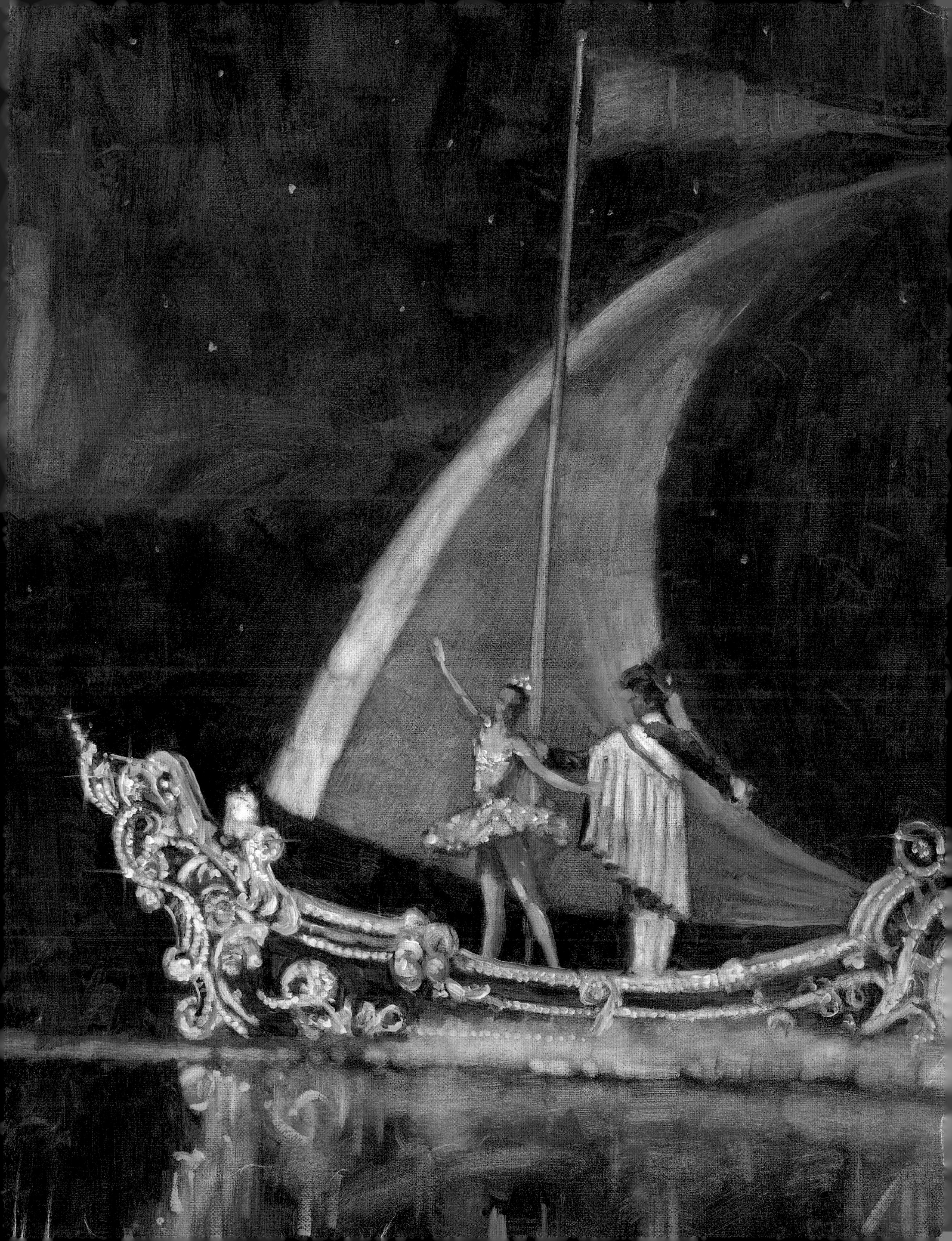

The Lilac Fairy shows him the way to the chamber of the sleeping princess. Florimund can hardly believe his eyes. "It is true," he seems to say, "the princess is real. At last, I have found her."

"Kiss her and she will awake," he is told. The prince kisses her softly and, in an instant, the cobwebs and dust disappear, and the great court of King Florestan comes to life. The guards and pages awaken; the king and queen open their eyes; the court stirs; and the beautiful princess rises slowly as the prince takes her into his arms.

CURTAIN

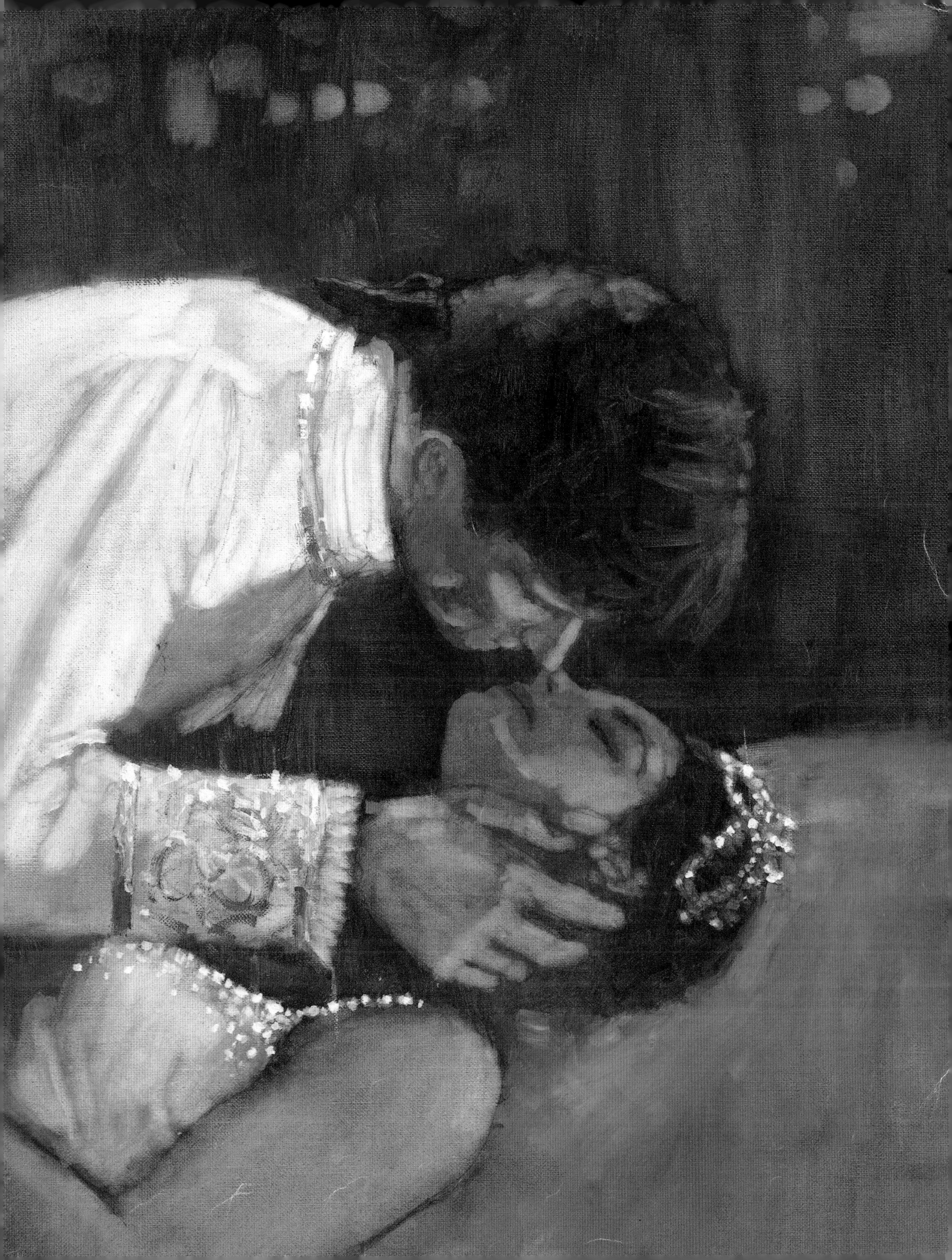

THE WEDDING

The scene sparkles with flowers, bright lights, and glorious court costumes. The king and queen are dressed in their finest, and even old Cattalabutte is a sight to behold. He announces all the guests as they enter, bow, and leave to prepare for their dances of celebration.

When everyone is in place, Aurora's brother and sisters perform a pas de quatre, a dance for four people. He is dressed as gold, his three sisters as a diamond, a ruby, and an emerald.

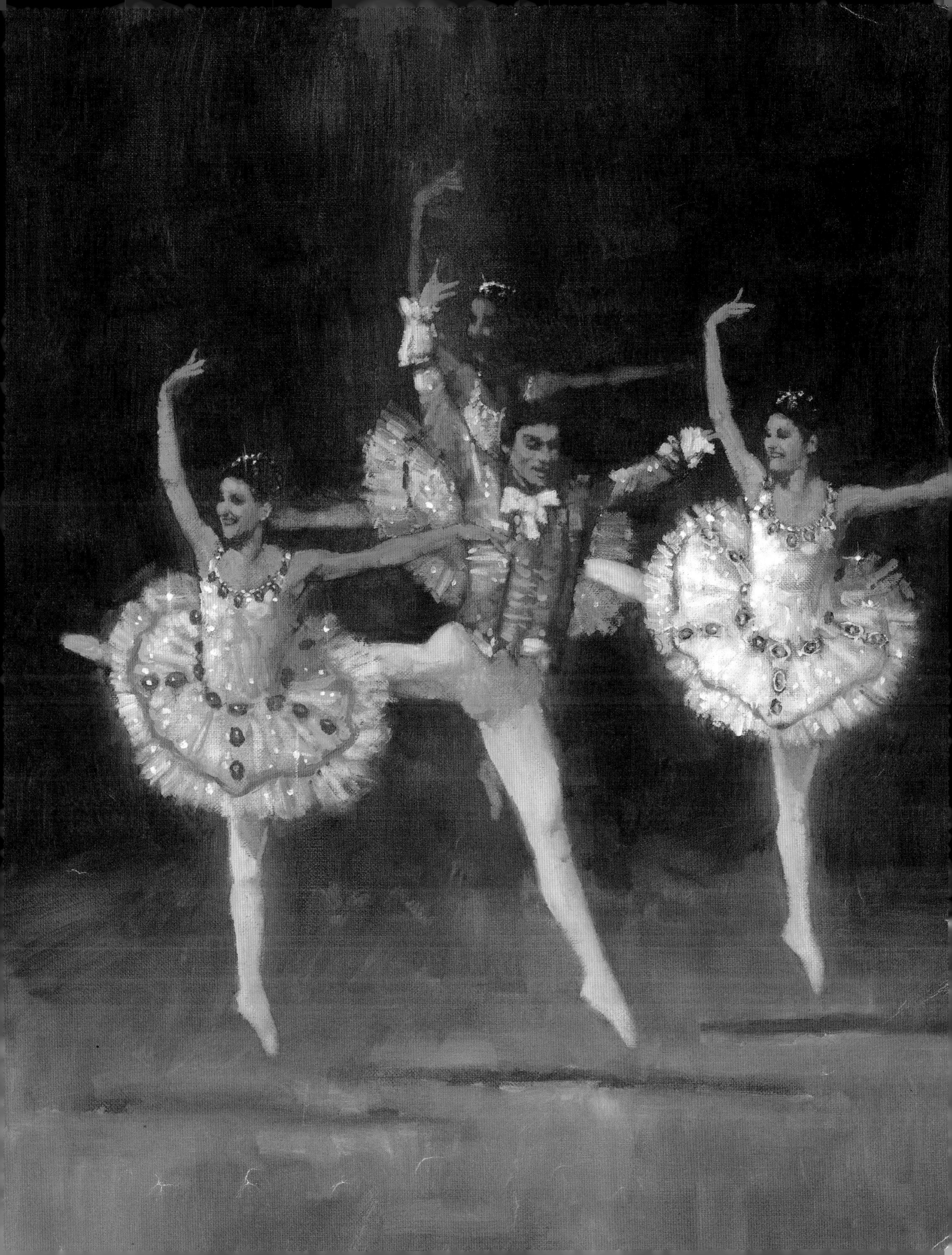

An oboe sounds meows for the next dancers: Puss in Boots and his companion, the White Cat.

Princess Florine, Aurora's sister, dances with a bluebird. He flutters his arms and beats his feet as he seems to fly into the air.

Little Red Riding Hood and the Wolf dance a familiar story, followed by three court jesters, who perform a rollicking Russian dance.

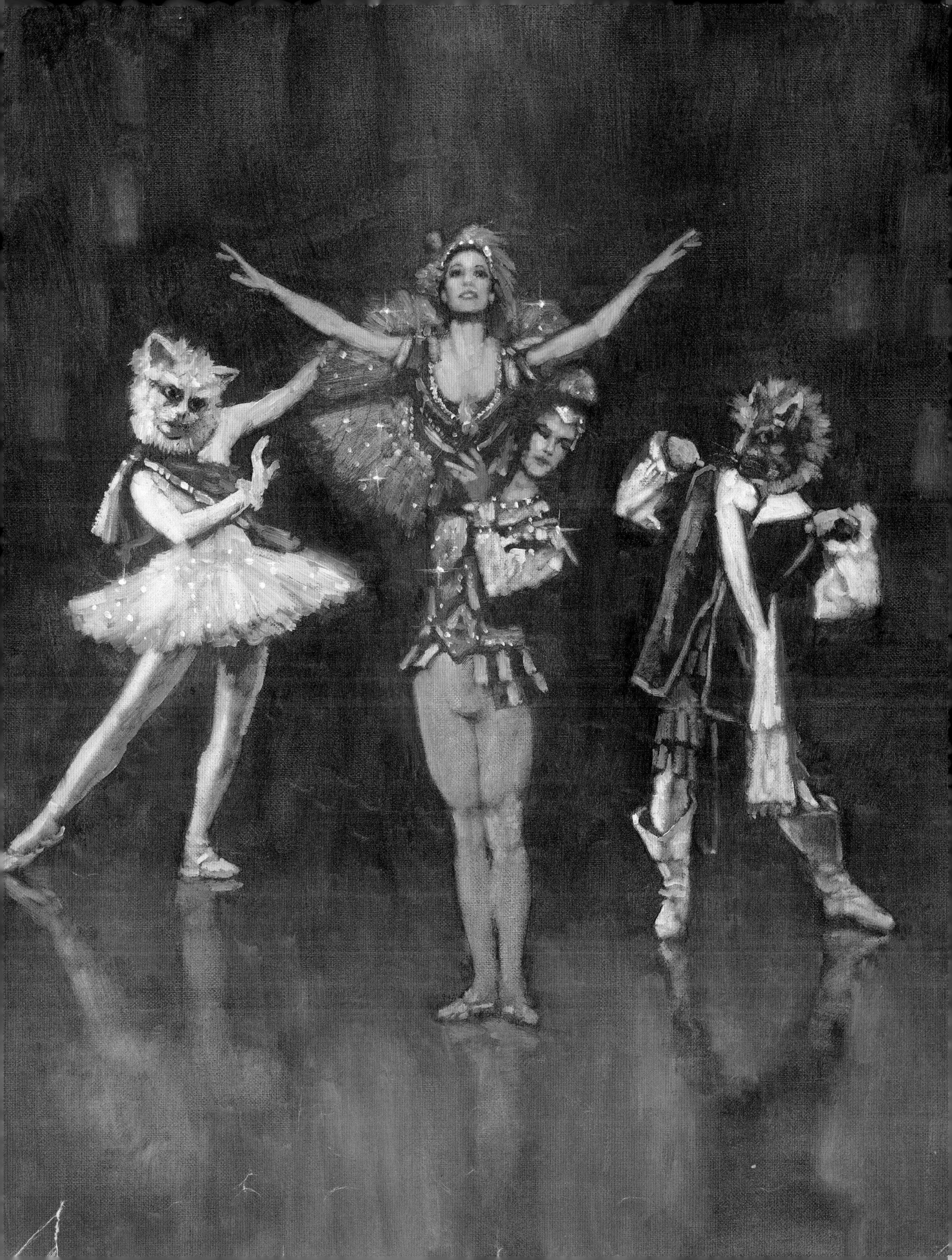

And then the big moment arrives: Prince Florimund and Princess Aurora enter, both dressed in dazzling white costumes. Aurora's dress is covered with radiant jewels, and on her head she wears a tiny crown.

She is no longer a bubbling sixteen-year-old princess, but a poised and elegant bride. The prince, too, dances with new confidence and gallantry, and he is no longer sad. The celebration ends with everyone dancing a dazzling Polish mazurka.

The princess and prince embrace and are surrounded by the fairy-tale figures, the fairy godmothers, and the entire court. And all will live happily ever after.

CURTAIN

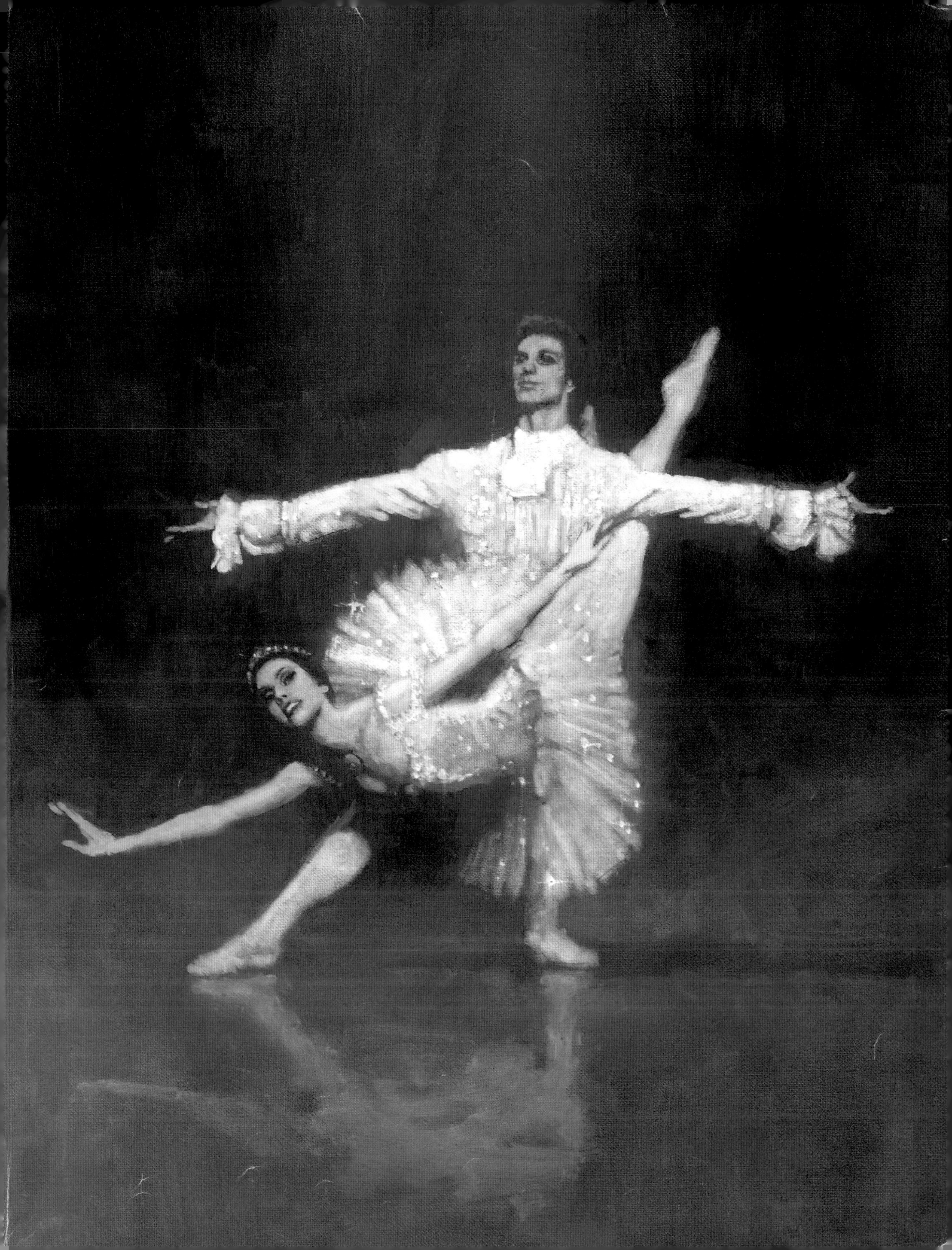

Atheneum
Macmillan Publishing Company
866 Third Avenue
New York, NY 10022

Maxwell Macmillan Canada, Inc.
1200 Eglinton Avenue East
Suite 200
Don Mills, Ontario M3C 3N1

Macmillan Publishing Company is part of
the Maxwell Communication Group of Companies

First edition
Printed in Singapore on recycled paper

10 9 8 7 6 5 4 3 2 1

The text of this book is set in 12 pt. Berkeley Old Style.
The illustrations are rendered in oil paints.

Library of Congress Cataloging-in-Publication Data

Horosko, Marian.
        Sleeping beauty : the ballet story / retold by Marian Horosko ;
    illustrated by Todd L. W. Doney.—1st ed.
              p. cm.
        Adaptation of : Spíaschaía krasavítsa.
        Summary: Presents the story of the ballet based on Perrault's fairy tale.
        ISBN 0-689-31885-5
        1.   Sleeping beauty (Choreographic work)—Juvenile literature. [1. Sleeping beauty (Ballet)
    2. Ballets—Stories, plots, etc.] I. Doney, Todd, ill. II. Tchaikovsky, Peter Ilich, 1840–1893.
    Spíaschaía krasavítsa. III. Title.
    GV1790.S55H67 1994   93–14399
    792.8'4—dc20